WOODY AND JUNE VERSUS THE IMPOSSIBLE CHOICE

WOODY AND JUNE VERSUS THE IMPOSSIBLE CHOICE

WOODY AND JUNE VERSUS THE APOCALYPSE, EPISODE 14

ROBERT J. MCCARTER

LITTLE HUMMINGBIRD PUBLISHING

Woody and June versus the Impossible Choice

Woody and June versus the Apocalypse, Episode 14

Copyright © 2023 by Robert J. McCarter

Except as permitted under the Copyright Act of 1976, this book may not be reproduced in whole or in part in any manner.

This book is a work of fiction. Names, places, and incidents are either products of the author's imagination or used fictitiously. Any resemblance to actual events or persons, living or dead, is entirely coincidental.

Cover photography © Robert J. McCarter

"Zombies Ahead" image by ducu59us

Version 1.0, February 2024

ISBN: 978-1-963354-01-0

Find out more about this book at: WoodyAndJune.com

Visit Robert's website at: RobertJMcCarter.com

Published by:

Little Hummingbird Publishing

P.O. Box 23518

Flagstaff, AZ 86002

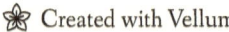 Created with Vellum

WOODY AND JUNE
VERSUS
THE APOCALYPSE

WOODY AND JUNE VERSUS THE APOCALYPSE

There are currently 17 episodes of *Woody and June versus the Apocalypse,* but episodes are collected into novel-length volumes with a larger story arc. This is the most economical way to consume these stories:

- Woody and June Versus the Apocalypse: Volume 1 (Episodes 1 - 7)
- Woody and June Versus the Apocalypse: Volume 2 (Episodes 8 - 12)
- Woody and June Versus the Apocalypse: Volume 3 (Episodes 13 - 17)

To stay abreast of all things Woody and June, head over to *Woody AndJune.com* and sign up for my e-mail newsletter so you don't miss out on a thing! Plus, you'll get a free ebook that includes "Park's Law of the Apocalypse," a newsletter-exclusive story in the world of Woody and June.

CHAPTER ONE

THE THREE OF US, June, Dallas, and I, are staring at a paved, two-lane road running through the Arizona desert, eyeing it like it might hurt us, like it's a dangerous thing. And that's probably good, because this is the apocalypse and roads are where people are and people are dangerous. Not to mention the zombies.

The spring afternoon is hot and it's been two days since we left the honeypot trap that Talia set up for us out in the area of off-the-grid homes called the 40s northeast of Flagstaff.

Dallas is leaning on a gnarled wooden cane, the kind an old grandpa would use, that we scrounged along the way. Her right ankle is getting better, the swelling is down, but if she walks on it much, she'll end up lame again. A very bad thing to be in the apocalypse.

The cane is an odd contrast to the curvy thirty-something Dallas dressed in jeans and a grey T-shirt that hugs those curves. She brushes her shoulder-length brown hair out of her eyes and invokes the official word of the apocalypse. "Shit," she says. "I'm afraid of a goddamn road."

We've spent days either on foot or on dirt bikes winding over sketchy, barely-there dirt roads or going overland to get here and now we need to get on a real road if we are to continue.

"Means you're not stupid," June says.

June is petite and athletic with ocean-blue eyes and short dark hair. She's in her mid-twenties, like I am, and is beautiful with olive skin and a cute turned-up nose and looks like the kind of young woman you would hire to play an elf at Christmas. Except, she's an ex-army badass and the love of my life.

A love I only discovered thirty-eight days ago, long after the zombies came and the world went to shit.

I've started to think of the place our relationship is in terms of gears. Right now it's in neutral. The affection and attraction are there, but we are still too deep into survival mode for it to get any traction.

This particular paved road is Arizona State Route 64 and it goes to the Grand Canyon. It's decision time. Do we go to the Canyon, try to help the survivors there against Talia and her minions, or do we get on these dirt bikes and ride as fast and as far as we can away from here?

Talia is a psychotic, petty, wannabe warlord well on her way to becoming a real warlord, and she just happens to be June's ex. You would think that the apocalypse would have taken care of all the crazy exes, but you would be wrong.

June is convinced that Talia wants us to go to the Canyon, wants us to meet her in battle, wants to defeat us in every way possible or die a warrior's death. This puts June in the position of killing or being killed by her former lover.

You see, June committed the cardinal sin for someone as petty and psychotic as Talia. She rejected her, multiple times, once by faking her death via zombie, the second by picking me over her. And I guess if we are really counting it up, there is a third time where June threatened to blow her head off if Talia didn't release me and Dallas.

The sun is high above us and I adjust the baseball cap on my head. The same place we scrounged the cane, we found some hats. This one is dark blue and is a touristy Grand Canyon hat. I miss my red Diamondbacks hat, but at least I got rid of that stupid straw hat and can look more like myself while I avoid getting too sunburned.

The road here is two-lane blacktop with that distinct post-apoca-lyptic look to it. Dirt and dried grass cover the blacktop and it looks like the land is trying to reclaim the road. And, of course, it is. Roads like this will only get worse from here.

I look around us at the fairly flat, very dry desert. As spring has progressed, what green grass there was has dried to straw-yellow, the only little bits of green left are small, thorny desert weeds. The dirt here is light with just a touch of red. To the east, in the distance, are the metal towers of high-tension power lines and to the west there's a low mesa sitting on the horizon. The road here is very straight, and despite being able to see a long ways, we are all still nervous.

We have the dirt bikes, we could continue going cross country, but we don't have a lot of gas left. We started with two jerry cans full of the proper gas and oil mixture for these two-stroke engines, but now there is just the one strapped to the handlebars of the bike I'm riding and it's not full anymore.

Besides, as we gain in elevation and the topography gets more complicated, using the dirt bikes will get harder and slower. There are a few dirt roads, but not for much longer and the dust would just attract more attention.

But the issue is we haven't actually made a decision yet. Do we go to the Grand Canyon or do we run? We headed north for the last few days mostly to get clear of Winslow and Flagstaff where Talia has taken over, but now we really needed to decide.

I look to the south, the way we came. I know we've been moving too fast for them to keep up, but I keep expecting the zombie pod that had been following us while we were on foot to crest the horizon.

Yes, I said following us, not attacking us. The zombies' group mind seems to have extended beyond their cooperative fresh brains radar—the more Zs the farther their range in detecting the living—into actual intelligence.

At Talia's honeypot out in the 40s, after we watched the pod take on fresh Zs, I approached them and yelled, "What do you want?" and the old Z at the center of the pod revealed herself and actually stared at me instead of looking through me like Zs usually do. They didn't attack. She held eye contact for a while and then they shambled away. This changed everything.

We now believe this pod behavior is happening everywhere and Zs will no longer be endless hunger and need personified, but endless hunger and need personified with added intelligence and cooperation. A zombie group mind fueled by the fungus that has taken them over.

Just thinking about the Zs makes the scratches on my arms and hands that I got in Winslow itch like mad. It's only been eleven days, but these scratches aren't healing normally, still angry and red, and they are driving me nuts.

"We need to decide," I say, ignoring the scratches and looking back at June and Dallas. The dirt bikes are sitting just off the road and we are standing on it. "We have to assume this road is watched. Either by the survivors down at Phantom Ranch or by Talia's people."

"And neither will likely look kindly on us," Dallas says, kicking at the dust and bits of dried vegetation on the road.

"There are some dirt roads," I say, "but I am not familiar with them and our dust will attract a lot of attention. Going overland will get impossible at points and we probably don't have enough gas. Desert View Overlook is around forty miles away, not long if we can use the road."

"Where else can we go from here?" June asks. She's quiet, not looking at either of us. She wants the fight, maybe as much as Talia does. After what Talia put us through in her sick little "game," I can't say that I blame her.

"North towards Page," I say. "We'd have to find gas and oil to get that far, but we could double-back to the North Rim and hike down the Canyon that way. Or we could head into Utah, there's Zion and the Virgin River, that could be a good place to hole up. Would be surprised if there aren't survivors there already."

June sighs and kicks at the pavement without looking up. Dallas is facing another direction doing pretty much the same thing.

We need a plan. We need shelter. But June wants to fight and Dallas wants to run and I don't know what I want.

Well... let me correct that statement. What I want is a safe place to hole up and try to survive this madness. A place where we can grow food and there is water. A place safe enough so June and I can resume our relationship. A place where we can welcome other sane survivors.

The problem is that Phantom Ranch at the bottom of the Grand Canyon near the Colorado River and next to Bright Angel Creek is just that kind of place. It is remote and defensible. It's got a long growing season and plentiful water. And Talia used to be in charge there and we are quite sure she's coming to take it back after she deals with some local conflicts in Flagstaff.

Talia is not the only psychotic, petty, wannabe warlord. The apocalypse has been fertile ground for the proliferation of them.

The last time June and Dallas had this discussion, it turned into a fight and it seems they are both avoiding it. But we can't just stand here.

"You still want to fight," I say to June.

"Yes," she says with a sharp nod.

"You still want to run," I say to Dallas.

"Right-o," she says. "Talia wants this fight and I don't want a thing that bitch wants."

"Then we head north," I say. They both turn and look at me, questions on their faces. "If we decide to fight, I think hiking down from the North Rim is a better bet. It's very unlikely Talia has any people there. And if we decide to run, we are farther away from Flagstaff."

"You should face facts, Woody," Dallas says, her arms crossed. "I'm not changing my mind and neither is she. Your dream of keeping the band together just ain't gonna happen."

"To go north, we have to get on 89 to cross the Little Colorado

River at Cameron," I say, ignoring Dallas. She's probably right, but keeping our group together seems more important to me than fighting or running. "We've driven through before without a problem, but things might have changed."

"Whatever..." Dallas says.

Silence descends. We are in a remote part of Arizona, so silence was always available in between cars zooming down the road, but this is the silence of the apocalypse we are talking about, and it's thick and deep, and while I often don't mind it, right then it bugs the hell out of me.

"June?" I ask.

She turns and faces me, her face serious. "Do you want to fight?" she asks, her voice quiet and her tone flat. "I need to know, Woody."

I open my mouth to speak, but I don't have the words. This feels like it's not just about making a stand against Talia but about our relationship and if it has a future.

"Because, if you don't," June continues, "you and Dallas should go north. Now. Get the hell out of here."

Now they are both staring at me and I am having trouble thinking. This is about our relationship. Not just June and me, but Dallas and me, and June and Dallas. June and Dallas know what they want, but I don't.

Not in this context.

"'Want' is a strong word when it comes to facing Talia," I say. Surprise ripples through June's face, for just a moment, and then it hardens into a tight-lipped frown. I keep talking, hoping it makes sense. "And I don't want to go to war with anyone." June's face tightens more. I'm not doing a good job of this. I start pacing down the road so I don't have to keep seeing her face.

"Does Talia need to be stopped?" I ask. "Yes. Of course. Do you know her better than anyone and have some advantage facing her? Yes. Are we equipped and prepared to take her on with a respectable chance of survival? No, not yet."

When I turn back around I'm about ten yards away. I see surprise on Dallas's face that quickly disappears, and June now has her arms crossed and is facing away from me.

I'm telling her the truth here. I owe it to her and I owe it to Dallas.

"Do I want to fight?" I say, walking back towards them. "No. Am I willing to fight to get us to safety? Of course."

I end up standing a few feet away from both of them, the three of us forming a triangle. Dallas is staring at me, but her face is passive and I can't tell what she is thinking. June is still looking away.

June strides to her bike, gets on, and kicks it to life.

I step towards her and open my mouth to say something, but the hard look on her face stops me. She shakes her head and rides away. To the west. Towards the Grand Canyon.

CHAPTER TWO

I'VE SAID it before and I'm sure I'll keep saying it. I don't understand women.

Standing there on Arizona State Route 64, the rumble of June's dirt bike quickly fading into the distance, I sure as hell don't understand June.

I guess it's a good thing for humanity that love can happen without understanding. Because I do love her. I don't want to be in this insane world without her. And I don't want to be in this insane world without Dallas either.

When June and I met at that dog food plant in Flagstaff, we were both go-it-alone survivors. Things have gotten crazy since we met, but it's been worth it. My life isn't just about my survival anymore. I'm not alone anymore. But June is alone now and she did it by choice, something I am having trouble grasping.

I look at Dallas and all of that must have been written on my face.

"Goddamn it," she says, but there's not much energy to it. "You know we have to go after her, so let's just go."

"But... you want to run," I say.

Dallas just shakes her head. "Shut up, Woody, and start the bike.

At least now we know what direction we are going." She walks over to the remaining dirt bike, takes off her pack, straps her cane to it, puts it back on, and stares at me with a quirky smile on her face.

See, I don't understand women. Not June riding off like that, not Dallas easing into this change so gracefully.

June and Dallas have been sharing the dirt bike, with Dallas in back. June made it look easy, but I know it's not and I still have the jerry can filled with gas tied to the handlebars. Not exactly ideal circumstances for a chase.

And we don't have helmets, not that that matters that much. Any wreck at a decent speed could injure you enough so that the apocalypse is no longer survivable. Dallas's twisted ankle would have been enough if she had been alone.

The bike is still warm, so it roars to life with one kick and Dallas climbs on the back.

"I'm sorry," I say as I sit on the bike and she wraps her arms around my waist.

"Shut up, Woody, and ride," she says, adding a whoop and holding me tighter.

And I kind of get it. With us being stuck in the cell tower treehouse and then the slow traversal over the desert, things have been kind of slow for the apocalypse. While life-threatening exploits are scary as hell, you sure do feel alive.

I take off my hat and shove it under my leg. I don't want to lose it. I click the bike into gear with my toe and ease us onto the blacktop. And then I give it some gas and start clicking up through the gears, the rumble of the engine through the frame and the seat joins the wind hitting my face and playing with my short brown hair.

"Here we come, June!" Dallas shouts from behind me. "We love you, you crazy bitch, and you don't get to do this alone!"

She laughs, a full-body laugh, and it's contagious and I laugh too. It's not the mwahahas of a psychotic, petty, wannabe warlord, nor is it the genuine laughter of a good joke. In fact, it sounds a little crazy mixing with the roar of the bike, but I'll take it. If nothing else, we laughed today and what is left on my list for this day is to survive and to spend time with June.

I give it a little more gas and the desert starts to blur around us and Dallas shouts "Yes!" as we roar down the road after June.

CHAPTER THREE

WOULD you die for someone you love?

This, of course, is a question that existed pre-apocalypse, to a greater or lesser degree depending on where you lived. If you lived in a first-world country like the United States, for many of us, it was to a lesser degree.

Now, since the Zs came, this is the kind of question you have to answer all the time, provided you are lucky enough to find love after the apocalypse.

I'm not talking about romantic love here, or sex, I'm talking about love in the purer sense of the word, where love means you care for someone else more than you care for yourself.

This is an important distinction. I'm sure in Talia's twisted narcissistic brain, she thinks she loves June, but I can assure you she doesn't care for June's well-being a fraction of how much she cares for her own.

I love June, with all the romantic stuff on top. And I love Dallas, with a more familial, big-sister kind of love, but love nonetheless.

And Dallas loves June, and it is not my place to categorize it more than that, but it is clear that there is love there.

Dallas and I speeding down Arizona State Route 64 on a buzzing dirt bike is us risking our lives to try to help June.

Sure, it's not an absolutely pure expression of love. After only thirty-eight days since meeting June, I feel absolutely lost without her. I need her in ways that may not be entirely healthy. And for Dallas it's partially about the thrill of the ride.

But mostly, it's because our friend is in a bad place and is doing stupid things. So we are doing a stupid thing to try to stop her from doing more stupid things and are clearly answering the question, would we die for June?

Yes. We would.

As the desert blurs around us, the twisting cut of the Little Colorado River to our right, the land hilly to our left, the desert decorated with grass and bits of sage, I have to ponder what is going through June's head.

Did she think Dallas and I would slink off and not follow her? Does she think that taking Talia on alone is somehow better than the three of us staying together? Or is she in so much pain for her perceived responsibility for Talia that she's not really thinking and just reacting?

It doesn't matter. Love and need drive us forward.

I've been down Route 64 since the apocalypse and been on it enough times that I know it pretty well. Last time I was through, there were no major obstructions, so we go fast.

But no matter how fast I want to go, I know June is going faster. There's only her on the bike. There's no jerry can tied to the handlebars. And, let's face it, she's got her demons chasing her.

I flash back to day four of Woody and June versus the Apocalypse when I drove June down this road in our shiny "new when the apocalypse happened" black pickup truck.

She wanted me to prove my fungus theory of the apocalypse and we had been nearby in the desert while she taught me how to shoot.

It seems silly to feel nostalgia for a time just over a month ago, but things seemed a lot simpler then. It was just the two of us and I had that giddy sense of the first blush of love, multiplied by not being alone anymore and starting to have a little hope for the future.

As we head up a hill and gain elevation, the land changes with bushy junipers appearing and the sage getting bigger. The farther up we go the bigger the junipers get, turning into actual trees joined by a few piñons. This part of the drive has always fascinated me, how a small change in elevation has a major impact on the plant life.

Meeting June was like that for me, my life was no longer a desert but quickly turned into a hardy forest.

As the trees grow, our view becomes occluded. That's one thing about the desert, it may be harsh but you can see far most of the time, and that is comforting these days.

This time, as the trees get taller, I grow more nervous. If there is danger just off the road, we won't see it coming. June wouldn't have seen it coming.

I feel my body tense and the thrill of the speed leeches away. It seems that Dallas can feel it too—she stops the whoops and leans closer to me.

I slow down some when I see the entrance gate to the Grand Canyon in the distance. It's two covered lanes with small booths, the walls made of local sandstone. There is a blue minivan in the right-most lane, which I don't remember, leaving only one lane clear.

It could be nothing. It probably is nothing, but I switch to the left lane, the idea of being enclosed like that, even briefly, is unpalatable.

We zoom through without incident, but I don't feel relieved. We are nearly to the turnoff to Desert View Overlook and I don't know which way to go. Did June continue on to the Grand Canyon Village, or did she stop here?

There's a trailhead down into the Canyon farther west a little, but June and I never went there. The zombie tourist horde caught up to us here, at Desert View, and we bushwhacked our way down and over to Tanner Trail.

I slow down as the turn to Desert View approaches on our right.

"What's wrong?" Dallas asks, speaking loud enough so I can easily hear her over the bike.

"I don't know which way she went," I say.

"Gas," she says.

Of course. These dirt bikes don't have a huge range, and as hard as we just went for the last forty miles, we must be about out of gas. June would know that.

I also mentioned the Tanner Trailhead wasn't far from her. June would remember that. If you were in a hurry to get into the Canyon and had limited gas, that would be your best bet.

I give the bike some gas and we zoom off to the west.

CHAPTER FOUR

I DON'T KNOW if this reference will survive, or even make sense, but let me give it a shot. In 1985, a movie called *National Lampoon's Vacation* came out. It starred Chevy Chase as a befuddled dad trying to take his family on a vacation and absolutely everything goes wrong.

There's a brief scene at the South Rim of the Grand Canyon right outside the El Tovar Hotel. Things have not been going well and, as I recall, there is a dead body strapped to the top of their station wagon.

The family rushes out to the rim and Chevy's character says, "Well we've seen it, now let's go."

Well... he said something like that. I'm sure DVDs of it still exist, but I don't have one handy to play it and check for accuracy.

Anyway, the joke is, under the right circumstances, even the majesty of the Grand Canyon isn't a big deal.

It was a joke I appreciated but not one I ever believed. This was a sacred place to my father and that rubbed off on me. The majesty of the millennia's long work of the Colorado River and the rain and wind, the geological record with all its color and beauty exposed, the sheer size of it and how it always seemed to put my problems in perspective.

As we roll into Lipan Point and get our first good look at the Grand Canyon, that joke from that old movie finally makes more sense. I see the majesty of the Canyon under a clear blue sky, the colors of the carved rock from taupe to salmon, the undulating layers of complexity in the eroded land, the winding Colorado River as it changes from meandering south to diving into the deeper canyon to the west. I take a deep breath of the warm air and feel the buzzing of my body from the long ride, but it's more, "Yeah, there's the Canyon, it's amazing, where the hell is June?"

The trailhead is off the road to the right before you get to the parking area and the actual point. It's easy to miss if you're in a hurry, and I am in a hurry.

I realize my mistake and curse, head farther into the oval, and back out to the road. There are a few long-abandoned cars here but no signs of recent activity and no Zs. The zombie tourist horde did, after all, follow June and me down into the canyon and it probably hasn't been long enough for another group to form.

That horde had been the old stupid variety of Zs, not at all like the pod that chased us. And good thing, or there never would have been a Woody and June versus the Apocalypse. At least not one worth writing about given that we would have been zombies ourselves and I don't think I would have had the interest or the dexterity to write.

I zoom around the oval, mostly ignoring the canyon, and get us back to the trailhead. Sure enough, June's dirt bike is there. The trail starts out steep with a two-panel display about the hike off the road a bit. The dirt bike is down past the signs on its side. Seeing it that way hits me hard for some reason. It's like the bike is a sick horse or something or maybe it's just the lack of June.

I thumb the kill switch, toe down the kick stand, shove my hat on, and run down to the bike, putting my hand near the engine.

"It's still warm," I say, looking back up to Dallas. There's a smile on my face, but I'm pretty sure it's one of the scary variety. My heart is pounding hard and a trickle of sweat is running down my temple.

"Awesome!" Dallas says with a smile, still sitting on the bike. "Go get her!"

My sweat goes ice cold and I get up and take a step towards Dallas. She can't make this hike. She's injured and couldn't outrun the Zs for very long at this point.

I take another step towards Dallas and her smile melts away as she sees the expression on my face.

"No," she says, shaking her head, her brown hair swishing over her shoulders. "Just go, Woody. Please."

This is why June left us like this. She figured I wouldn't be able to leave Dallas injured, and I can't.

Dallas's words from earlier today come back to me, "Your dream of keeping the band together just ain't gonna happen."

But it was June that broke us up. It was June that left. She left us. It was June that left me.

I turn back and look at the bike. I can see fresh footprints going down the trail. I know where she is going. She didn't know the trailhead was two overlooks west of Desert View and probably wasted time at Navajo Point and is probably not that far ahead. I might be able to catch up with her.

Chevy Chase's character was right. As I stare down the trail, I don't even care about the view. Not one bit.

CHAPTER FIVE

LIFE WAS ALWAYS full of impossible choices and an uncertain future. The apocalypse has just magnified it. Staying with Dallas or going after June was one of those impossible choices.

The apocalypse is also all about fight or flight. If you were prone to freeze you probably didn't make it very far into the world of Zs.

But right then on the very beginning of Tanner Trail at Lipan Point on the South Rim of the Grand Canyon on a warm spring day, I freeze.

I know that not making a choice is still a choice, although I have never liked that phrase, true as it may be. It denies the very real situations where a choice can be quite impossible.

I hear ravens cawing in the distance and the gentle rustle of the juniper trees from the breeze, but louder than all of that is my heart clanging in my head. My sweat is cold and my mouth is dry.

I should move. I need to move.

Either go after June or go back to Dallas and find some shelter.

But I can't do either, so I stand there, my brain in neutral, frozen.

It's not safe. The zombies have grown a brain, and despite the tourist zombie horde chasing June and me into the Canyon, a new pod could have formed.

Talia's game was terrible and twisted and cruel, but what June just did was terrible too. Did she even think about how it would affect me?

Yes, of course she did. She knew I wouldn't be able to leave an injured Dallas. She knew what this would do to me and left anyway. Even then, I know she was trying to save me from this war with Talia. After I had told her the truth about my hesitation she must have concluded this was her only course.

But that doesn't make it right. That's not the way you treat those you love.

"Woody," Dallas says gently.

She's right next to me, having gotten off the bike, gotten her gnarled wood cane out, and hobbled down to me without me even noticing.

I blink and look at her. "I... I can't... I..." I mumble, my thoughts far from coherent.

"You need to go after her," she says, her tone gentle again. "You need to go now."

"But... I... You..." I say, not even able to put two words together.

"You told me about Desert View," she says, "and the tower there. I can get the bike in second gear and get myself back there and hole up. Let my ankle heal."

I'm staring at her, aware that I'm blinking too much, my brain still stuck in neutral.

"I'm sorry about this," Dallas says, but her tone isn't so gentle anymore. I don't have time to puzzle it out because she slaps me. Hard. My head snaps to the side and my right cheek lights up with fiery pain.

"Shit!" I cry. "What the hell was that, Dallas? You didn't need to —" I cut myself off, because I realize that she did need to. My heart is beating harder, but at least I can form an entire sentence.

"All those scribblings you keep doing," she says, referring to my diaries. "It's 'Woody and June' versus the Apocalypse. Go get her."

"She left me," I say, hating the pleading tone of my voice, like I'm some child.

"She loves you, and as stupid as it was, she's trying to protect you." Her mouth quirks into a smile and adds, "And me. But you know what? Screw that. We make our own choices, Woody. We live and we die by them. And my choice is to get to the top of the tower and heal up. Maybe work on my suntan."

I look down the trail and I know that after twenty-eight days with Dallas it will be so strange not to have her around. But on the other hand, I can't imagine my life without June. And, besides, if I insist on going with Dallas, waiting in the tower until she's healed, she will be so mad at me she will make my life a living hell.

"I'll come back for you," I say.

She tilts her head to the side and stares at me for a moment and then shakes her head. "Don't make stupid promises, Woody. I'm only alive right now because of you and June. Because you didn't kill me even after you learned that I was doing the queen bitch's bidding and helping her capture you guys. You owe me nothing."

I open my mouth to say more, but can't find the words, this time for different reasons. But then Dallas is hugging me, hard, and there is no need for words and I just hug her back.

After a while I do find a few words. "You *are* my best friend," I say.

"Damn right," she answers and hugs me harder.

CHAPTER SIX

TANNER TRAIL IS OLD. In its current form, it has been in use since the late 1800s. Well... post-apocalypse it's not used very much, but it's most definitely still in use. This is about to become important.

Even before that, Native people used this route to get from the rim of the Grand Canyon to the Colorado River. At nine miles, it's a little bit longer than the more popular Bright Angel and Kaibab trails, but follows the natural contours of the land in a more straightforward way than the other trails.

The upper section of the trail follows a gully staying first on the east side and then switching to the west side, when the rock changes from the Toroweap Formation to Coconino Sandstone.

For the first part, if you are going down, you can easily lose the trail and stay on track. The trail is badly eroded in places and is often covered by rockslides, but the path essentially follows the drainage. At a certain point, a few miles down, as the trail hugs the Escalante Butte and then Cardenas Butte, if you keep following the drainage you will get in trouble, the drainage becoming unnavigable.

This is what I worried about as I hustled down the trail leaving Dallas behind. June didn't know this trail and could easily get lost in the Canyon. And, yes, we had bushwhacked our way down to the Tanner Trail from near the Desert View Overlook with the zombie tourist horde after us, but we had gotten lucky. The Grand Canyon is a dangerous place and you can't count on that kind of luck.

I didn't look back, I couldn't, but my shoulders relaxed a little when I heard the dirt bike start up behind me and heard Dallas whoop.

Setting off on a Grand Canyon hike when I was a kid was just about the most exciting thing I could think of. The view of the Canyon from the rim is spectacular, but it's kind of like the Cliffs-Notes version of the experience. As you descend down through the layers, down through the geological history of the planet and back in time, there are wonders to discover at every turn.

As I hustle down the trail, the majesty of the Canyon is not completely lost on me, but it is certainly a background thought. I'm more focused on keeping the fastest pace I can manage, one that is dialed back one notch from stupid.

This is rough terrain, with lots of loose rock and it would be easy to slip and fall. And in the state June is in, God knows what kinds of risks she is taking.

This is the apocalypse, there is no search and rescue to come after you, no helicopter available to swoop in and pull you out. Even a sprained ankle like Dallas got just outside of Winslow could mean the end, and a broken leg or ankle is a death sentence.

And I don't want to lose the trail. Risk goes way up, fast, once you are off the trail. I've been on this trail a number of times, I've studied the map of it fairly recently and done my fair share of hiking, but that doesn't make the trail hard to lose.

But what if June wandered off the trail? Should I scramble down the trail as fast as I can calling for her like she's some kind of lost dog? Or pretend I don't know the general contours of the trail and see where I lose it and figure that is where she will lose it.

No. June is capable and intelligent. June is athletic and in better shape than I am.

As the drop in elevation chases the junipers away and the land becomes more desertlike, I slow my pace back two notches from stupid and focus on keeping on the trail.

It's all I can do right now.

CHAPTER SEVEN

NINE MILES of hiking eleven days after succumbing to all the zombie scratches I got in Winslow with two days of walking thrown in between is not easy.

And you might think, hiking down is easier than hiking up. And it is aerobically, but it's not easier on your body. You need a whole different set of muscles to slow your descent, ones that aren't used very much and tire quickly.

I slow down when the trail is fairly even for a while, where it is pulling away from the gully and starting to hug Escalante Butte which rises almost a thousand feet to my left.

The soil of the butte must have plenty of iron, because it is red-tinged and has a series of triangular peaks giving it a decidedly Egyptian vibe. Not that I give it too much attention. I am focused on the trail, looking for signs of someone wandering off and continuing down the drainage towards danger.

But it's not like this is moist, loamy soil that easily holds footprints. This is the desert, the soil sandy, and staring at the ground, trying to see freshly scuffed dirt or a recently moved rock is something of a long shot.

At the trailhead, I was able to see the signs of June's recent passage. The soil there is loose and sandy and the slope steep. And, besides, I had the fresh motorcycle tracks to compare to. Here? It's nearly impossible. But it's worth it so I slow down and try.

I'm maybe three miles in and need to make wiser use of my energy anyway.

My thoughts drift back up the rim to Dallas. I hope that she got to the Desert View Watchtower. That she thought to hide the bike and is set for a few days of rest.

I'm desperate to find June. Not only because of what she means to me, but because I am worried about her state of mind with this whole Talia thing. It's complicated. But I miss Dallas in a simpler way. I miss her enthusiastic laughter and sharp wit. I miss her teasing and her impatience with my need to analyze pretty much everything. I miss her fiery temper and the energy it brought to a lot of low moments.

I don't even know her last name, but she is, literally, one of the most important people in the world to me.

You might not think that means much with there being so few people left and so few that I've been able to really spend time with lately. But it does. Dallas and I have been through a lot. The long hike from near the North Rim to Lees Ferry. The crazy rafting trip down the Colorado which was necessary but beyond stupid. The hike up this very trail to get back to our truck at Desert View so we could go back to Flagstaff and get supplies to rescue June and take on the psychotic, petty, wannabe warlord there. Not to mention rescuing June and getting her back from Talia at Phantom Ranch.

And that's the stuff just the two of us have done. When you consider what the three of us have done together, surviving this last month, it's pretty epic. The apocalypse has a way of compressing things, and as I desperately seek June, I miss Dallas. Badly.

As the trail completes its transition out of the drainage, I pause, take off my hat, and wipe the sweat from my forehead.

This isn't one of those jaw-dropping expansive views of the Canyon. To my left rises up Escalante Butte and to the right is the rim of the Canyon. It's an amazing view, world class really, but it's not like the full view of the Canyon—it's just a piece of it.

This is one of those views that you can't see from the rim, that you have to earn through hiking, one of the many details that unfold as you leave the CliffsNotes view from above and hike down.

High above me to the east is where the Desert View Watchtower is. I take a moment, scan the rim, and feel unexpected relief when I see the tower poking up above the horizon. I stare at it for a moment. I don't know if I expect Dallas to use a mirror and flash me some Morse code to let me know she is all right or something, but do I wish for it. She's family now and I miss her already.

Nothing happens, and with a little further reflection, I am glad. Even if she is scanning the trail and spots me with her binoculars, it wouldn't be wise to call attention to herself.

On a hopeful whim, I pull out my walkie-talkie, turn it on, and wave it in the air. The tower is only a mile or so away and we have a clear line of sight.

I stare at the tower for another minute and nothing happens. Suddenly I feel so very alone. I'm in the wilds of the Canyon by myself. That's never happened before. Even pre-apocalypse, it wasn't a good idea to hike by yourself. But more than that, after the mess in Phoenix, after all those months I spent on my own, after all the shit that went down there, I was certainly lonely, but I didn't feel this alone.

Back then I was alone on purpose. Because the psychotic, petty, wannabe warlord down there had gone too far. Because my inaction had cost two people I cared about their lives. Back then I was alone because I wanted to be alone.

Not now. I am alone by necessity.

I feel the weight of it as I stop waving the walkie and turn back to start walking down the trail, my heart heavy, and despair taking me over.

I won't find June. I'll never see Dallas again. And I'll die down here alone and become one of the stinking shamblers, forever haunting this canyon looking for human flesh to eat.

"About time, dummy," Dallas says from my walkie, more than a little laughter in her voice. "I've been waiting for you to turn it on since I spotted you twenty minutes ago."

I have written previously how hope can turn on a dime and become despair and that's why it's wise sometimes not to hope. Especially not now. Not in the apocalypse. But the opposite is true—despair can flip over to hope just as quickly.

"Dallas!" I say into the walkie, feeling the weight lifted, my despair turning to hope.

"Who the hell else would it be, genius?" she says. "Over."

"What can I say?" I say into the walkie. "I missed you, Dallas. Over."

"Missed me?" she asks. "Give me a break. I know I'm amazing and all, but it's only been an hour or so."

She doesn't say "over" so I don't say anything back right away and then she adds, "But, yeah, I kinda missed you too. Over."

CHAPTER EIGHT

I HIKE down the trail with renewed energy. Dallas can see much better than I can and is actively searching for June. Theoretically speaking, much of the Tanner Trail is visible from the Desert View Watchtower, but practically speaking it's a tiny trail in the vast Grand Canyon and following it with just a set of binoculars is not exactly easy.

But that's not what Dallas is doing. She's scanning the area for motion. For June. I spend quite a bit of time explaining the trail to Dallas, trying to orient her on the topology of this part of the Canyon and the path of the trail. From the rim down the gully, around the base of the two buttes, and then along a ridge above Tanner Canyon all the way down to the river.

Sounds simple enough, right? But a few words to describe the expanse of this magnificent canyon doesn't quite cut it. So we go back and forth—Dallas explains what she is seeing, and I try to visualize it and put it in context—all while I hustle down the trail.

The earth here is red-tinged, like the buttes above me, and there are low bush-like junipers, dried grasses, weeds and boulders of varying sizes, and not much else. It's genuinely hot and I'm very thirsty, but I have to ration my water until I can get to the river.

And that's the thing that makes the Grand Canyon so appealing right now. The Colorado River combined with the rugged landscape and remoteness. You have to really work to get here, but once you do, you have all the water you could possibly use.

Not that the river isn't a bit of a concern. The flow is controlled by Glen Canyon Dam which forms Lake Powell upstream. This is the apocalypse and I doubt that anyone is carefully monitoring water levels. What if something happens up there and the flood gates are suddenly opened?

I stop, dust puffing up around my feet and a few pebbles rolling away, as the thought settles in. I had imagined this an ideal place to survive, and it is, except for a looming existential threat like that.

I shake it off. It's ten steps down the road and requires us getting the band back together, talking the Phantom Ranch survivors into letting us help them, and then surviving Talia and her minions.

What're the odds of some system failing at the dam or some curious numbskull exploring the place and pressing the wrong button?

And there is probably a group of survivors up there. Because they not only have water, they have plentiful electricity if they can keep the place running.

I file the thought away in a hopeful to-do list for the far future. Something like, "Send scouting party to the Glen Canyon Dam and assess."

I guess this comes with being alone and not having my life under immediate threat of termination. I haven't had the space for these kinds of musings in a while and I kind of like it.

This is, ideally, what will happen in the future. Groups of survivors finding a place where they can make a stand and then slowly exploring and finding other survivors, trading with each other, and gradually reweaving the fabric of society.

It's a nice thought but it doesn't account for the psychotic, petty, wannabe warlords and the newly intelligent zombie pods. Either of those will make reweaving the fabric of society difficult, but both will make it nearly impossible.

"I see her!" Dallas says over the walkie, her voice bright with excitement. "I see June!"

This news, along with my musing of a survivable future, collide and I feel a burst of happiness, true happiness. I am hopeful and excited and eager for the future.

Yeah, I know, June left us knowing how it would affect us. Let me say that more clearly. June left *me* knowing how it would affect *me*. I shouldn't speak for Dallas. And, yeah, that is there in the background, but the happiness and the hope swamps over it.

I give Dallas a moment and she doesn't say "over" so I figure she is too excited. "Where is she?" I ask. "How far ahead? Over."

"A few miles at least," Dallas says. "Past the buttes where the trail climbs out of the Tanner Canyon and starts riding along the ridge. That's why I didn't see her for a bit, she was on that section of the trail. Over."

I'm standing still, Dallas's words washing over me, a silly grin on my face, and then the smile melts away and I flick the button on the walkie. "Are you sure it's her? Over."

"What the hell do you mean," Dallas says. "Of course I'm sure it's..." There's a pause as if she hadn't even considered it, as if she had seen someone on the trail and assumed it was June, as if she just realized just like I had that lucky breaks don't happen very often in the apocalypse.

"Yeah..." she continues. "Rifle sticking up out of the backpack. Short, dark hair. I mean she's a long ways away, but it has to be her, Woody. It has to be—"

The channel is still open, and her pause makes my sweat turn icy. I want to say something, but I know she won't even hear it.

"Shit!" Dallas says. "There's Zs, about six of them, and they are... Shit! They are trying to sneak up on her. They aren't acting normally. They are a goddamn pod."

CHAPTER NINE

THIS IS why you don't split up. This is why you stay together. A couple of days ago if you had asked me if I was worried about June taking on six Zs in the open, I would have laughed. June would take them every time.

Now that the Zs have grown a brain, now that Dallas just confirmed this wasn't an isolated thing with the Zs that were under our cell tower treehouse for those five days, I just don't know. The game has changed now that the stinking embodiments of eternal hunger and unquenchable need are not just single-minded, stupid eating machines.

I start jogging down the trail as fast as I safely can, with the backpack bouncing on my back. Sure, June is a couple of miles ahead of me, sure it will make no difference in the fight she is about to find herself in, but it's all I can do.

"Shit! There's more in front of her," Dallas says, "but they seem less organized. No... no way. They are pretending to be stupid Zs, giving those behind her time to close in. Shit! Shit! Shit!"

Forget jogging, forget safety, I start running. It takes everything I have to not just shuck the backpack so I can go faster. But that would be stupid, and a very annoying part of my brain does the math. Two miles on rough territory, the best speed I could probably manage would be ten-minute miles, if that, putting me twenty minutes off.

This battle is only going to last minutes, how fast I run doesn't matter. I slow back down to a fast walk which will get me there in thirty-five or so minutes.

When I hear the sound of distant gunfire, I almost speed up again but then realize this is a good sign.

"She sees them," Dallas says over the walkie. "All of them. She is heading off the trail. Two are down."

The odds have shifted in June's favor. She's armed and more than competent with her firearms. Although it said something that she resorted to a gun. June knows firsthand how that kind of sound can travel down here and she knew she would be announcing her presence.

"They're not following," Dallas says. "The freaking Zs are not following her."

I stop again, the thoughts running through my head too potent. The Zs didn't follow June. They are waiting right by the trail for someone to hike by so they can attack from both directions. The Zs set a trap.

"Shit," I mumble. This is worse than I feared. A lot worse.

And this is happening all over the place right now. Up in that cell tower treehouse after we dropped our makeshift bomb on them, we got to witness them growing a brain. A few days later, I saw the old, desiccated Z out in the 40s at the center of the pod that had been following us and I got to feel her intelligence when she looked me in the eye. But the rest of the world? Do they know the Zs just grew a brain? How many more of the living will fall figuring this out?

I start moving again, walking as fast as I can. I've got to catch up with June. I just have to.

Ƙƛƛ Ȳ ƛƛƛ

AS I HUSTLE down Tanner Trail, my backpack bouncing gently along with my steps, I try to remember the portion of the trail where June was attacked by the intelligent pod.

The trail rides along the top of a ridge on one side of Tanner Canyon. The views are good and you can often get glimpses of the Colorado snaking through the Grand Canyon to the west. The South Rim rises up above you to the east, and to the north the canyon just seems to go on and on fading into the distance.

Because of the ridge the trail follows, it's not a good place to get off the trail. Actually, Tanner Trail is a fairly direct and well thought-out route. For where we are, it balances safety and expediency extremely well. It's why the use of this trail goes back so far.

I try to get in June's head. She's forced off the trail because of the Zs. She slips down off the ridge a bit because of the loose soil, her heart pounding, cursing because she too realizes that the Z-pod thing is not isolated. She can see the Colorado River to the west and knows that is the way she wants to go, where Phantom Ranch is. She knows she can't really get lost if she just heads west, but the terrain is barren and rough and unforgiving and it's by no means a straight shot, the dry, rocky land undulating up and down between her and the river.

She looks up and realizes that the Zs are not following her, that she can just parallel the trail for a bit and carefully get back on it. But now that she knows that Zs are capable of waiting in ambush, she knows there could be more. The choice is to brave going west without a trail or get back on the trail and risk more attacks.

In my imagination, June pauses, catching her breath and considering it. She looks back over the rough land to the west and again sees the gleaming promise of water. She looks back up towards the rim and thinks about me, wishing I were there, knowing that I am familiar with this area and could assess the difficulty of leaving the trail better. She's missing my calm presence and my warm embrace. She's thinking of my broad shoulders and passionate kisses. She licks sweat off her upper lip and wipes her beautiful black hair away from her brow, her ocean-blue eyes wishing they could see me, longing for me.

I start laughing as I walk down the trail a few miles away from June. The first part of that thought experiment, trying to get into her head and think through her choice, was useful. The second part? Not so much.

I am sure June is having thoughts of me. And I doubt they have anything to do with my broad shoulders or passionate kisses. I don't know what her thoughts might be, but I am sure they are complicated.

"She's back on the trail," Dallas says over the walkie. "About a hundred yards down from where she was attacked. She's definitely slowed her pace down. Now's your chance, lover boy."

Dallas doesn't say "over" and a moment later I hear her laughter coming through. "Sorry, sorry," she says. "But any laughter in an apocalypse, isn't that what you say, Woody? Over."

My cheeks feel hot and not just from the Arizona sun. "That's what I say. Over." I quicken my pace as much as I dare. I know where the Zs are and don't have to worry about them for a couple of miles.

"I hope it's a happy reunion," Dallas says, still laughing. "Make it a good one for this old spinster, will ya? I'll be watching."

I just shake my head and keep going feeling hopeful and happy.

I should have known better.

Another voice comes over the walkie, one with a gentle southern accent that brings with it a rush of adrenaline. "I'll be watchin' too, Mr. Woodpecker. So, do make it a good reunion, because it's goin' to be your last."

Talia!

I turn and look back towards the Desert View Watchtower. Talia has to be on the rim for her to be involved in our conversation and there's only a few overlooks on this end of the Canyon and only one significant one.

"Dallas!" I shout into the walkie. "Run!"

A gleeful cackle comes over the walkie-talkie. "Too late, Mr. Woodpecker. Once again you are too damn late."

CHAPTER TEN

I FREEZE on the trail again, my heartbeat a rushing woosh in my head. June is close. There is a chance I could catch her. Dallas is farther away but in danger, this being the third time that Talia has caught Dallas since we met her. How can she possibly survive a third?

"Just run, Woody," Dallas says over the walkie, her voice serious. "Leave me. Run. Now!"

The walkie goes dead and I hear distant gunfire from the rim, but I can't move. I'm frozen again under the hot sun on the trail below Escalante Butte and above Tanner Canyon.

The apocalypse has presented me with many impossible days where my life was constantly on the line. This isn't one of those days, but it's a different kind of hell, one of impossible choices.

First, when June left, and now with Dallas.

But I'm several hours away from Dallas, and whatever is going to happen is going to happen without me. I can't change it. And that's the logic talking, telling me that I need to go after June, tell her what happened, have her help me get Dallas back.

But June left me. June is the reason we split up, the reason Dallas has no chance of fighting off Talia and her people, and I'm stuck here between the two of them frozen.

Logic is not enough to get me moving with my emotions in such turmoil.

For a brief moment, I wish that I hadn't ever met June at the dog food factory in Flagstaff. That I had stayed the go-it-alone survivor I had been for all those months. That Woody never had to face a situation like this because that Woody didn't have anyone alive that he truly cared about. Alive anymore, that is.

And that Woody would have probably died when he ran into the psychotic, petty, wannabe warlord encamped at the top of Mount Elden, so it's a silly thought and a transient one, but my mind is enough of a mess that it is one that I have.

"There are three rules to my game," Talia says over the walkie, the smugness in her voice making me want to hit her over and over. "One, I win. Two, the more you play, the longer Dallas-girl survives. Three, I win.

"And I must say, you all have been playing it very well, showing up here just as I planned. But, honestly, I didn't expect you all to split up, makin' this so easy for me."

I don't reply, anger giving me energy that I have nothing to do with.

"Cat got your tongue, Mr. Woodpecker?" she asks.

"I'm sorry," I say into the walkie, trying to keep my voice as calm as possible. "Perhaps you didn't know this, but it is customary to say 'over' to signal the other party when you are done talking since walkie-talkies don't support sending and receiving at the same time. I didn't think you were done talking, so as a basic courtesy I didn't say anything. *Over*."

When I release the button on the walkie-talkie, Talia is already talking, "...you little condescending prick. I'm going to tear you apart with my bare hands. So here's what's going to happen. You are going to march yourself back up here or Dallas dies. Turn around now or I'll put a bullet in her head myself." I hear a brief strangled cry from

Dallas like she's trying to say something but I can't make it out. "You have thirty seconds to comply."

The anger has burned away my hesitation and I can see clearly that if I go back, Talia will capture me too and use us both against June. And I can also see that if I don't go back Talia will probably kill Dallas, and nothing so clean as a bullet to the head.

It's an impossible choice but one I can actually make.

"No," I say into the walkie, letting my anger and energy feed into my voice. "Meet me alone on the Bright Angel Bridge in forty-eight hours. Bring Dallas with you and come unarmed and you and I can settle this once and for all. Over."

I'm staring at the tower on the rim, pretending I can see Talia and letting my hate show on my face. She's watching me, I know she is, and I don't know if she can see me clearly enough for it to matter, but I'm done with these games. I'm done letting her set all the conditions.

And, yes, Talia is trained in hand-to-hand combat and I am not. And, yes, the bridge is a terribly exposed location and I have little doubt that she will make sure I don't survive even if I do win the fight by some chance.

But forcing this confrontation on different terms is all I can do. Even if it means I die, I will not play her game anymore.

"Unless you are afraid," I say into the walkie. "Are you afraid of a fair fight with me, Talia? Over."

It takes longer than it should, but when I hear Talia again, she is laughing. "Oh, I'm sorry. You think that I don't control Phantom Ranch. You think that you can find some support down there. What the hell did you think I was doing when I left you all up that cell tower with a few thousand Zs to keep watch on ya?"

My anger drains and all that is left is cold fear, but I know I can't let that show. "I'll see you and Dallas in two days," I say and turn and start walking down the trail. "No Dallas, no fight. Over and out." I turn my walkie-talkie off, make a show of stuffing it in my backpack, and I don't look back.

CHAPTER ELEVEN

DALLAS'S LIFE relies on the ego of a narcissist, Talia, taking the bait I offered. If Talia can't let my challenge go and does take that bait, then my life relies on Talia having lied when she said that she already had control of Phantom Ranch.

In an arm-wrestling contest between Talia and me, I'm pretty sure I would win. I have more upper-body strength than she does with all the years with a bat in my hand, both pre- and post-apocalypse. But in a brawl? The odds are easily with Talia.

And I say that with no shame. She is taller than me, trained, and with a wiry strength that is easy to see. The odds are stacked against me and I am counting on her realizing that and her narcissistic ego not being able to let it go. How can she walk away from a fight with someone she hates and someone she believes she can easily defeat?

The answer to that question is she is very petty and very psychotic, so expecting her to be predictable is a bit problematic.

As I walk down the trail, I hear a single gunshot come from the rim. I flinch, but I don't break stride. That sound could signal Dallas's end or it could just mean Talia is desperate to get me to turn the walkie back on and engage in further conversation.

But that would be playing her game and I am done with that.

It takes everything I have not to turn around, not to slow down, but I don't. I keep walking down Tanner Trail. I keep my back straight and my head held high. I pray to a god I don't really believe in that Dallas is still alive, that this crazy thing I did will give us all a chance of survival. Somehow.

As I make my way along the base of Escalante Butte and then Cardenas Butte, my mind is in this strange state as my legs chew through the miles. I'm vaguely aware of the Canyon, how the layers unfold as I move down the trail, each turn revealing a new view. I'm also aware of the sun moving towards the west and the shadows starting to lengthen, of it getting hotter as I go down in elevation. I'm aware of my sweat, my shirt damp where the backpack sits on my shoulders and back. I'm aware of the breeze that comes and goes and cools me. I get thirsty and take a sip of water now and then without really thinking about it.

I am aware of all these things, but I am not truly aware of them at the same time, if you know what I mean. I am there and not there, my mind going over all that has happened in the last thirty-eight days since I met June and then Dallas. My mind is especially reviewing the last few days since we left the cell tower treehouse and headed back here with the intent of confronting Talia. It especially dwells on the challenge I made with Talia and the long odds of me surviving it and what it would take, what I might have to do, to survive.

That last thought haunts me because many of the things I might have to do to survive would change me and I don't want the apocalypse to change me like that. Don't get me wrong, it's changed me, a lot, physically, mentally, and spiritually. I don't want to become the kind of person that pre-apocalypse me wouldn't recognize, wouldn't like, would be afraid of.

What makes it complicated isn't what I would do for my own survival, but what I would do for June's survival and Dallas's survival. It's clear as I mull it over that I could justify a lot more if it's their lives on the line.

It's not your usual Grand Canyon hike, that's for sure.

When I get to the point in the trail where it dips down into Tanner Canyon, I remember the zombie pod ambush coming up. I even get my bat out and check the gun on my hip. I go through the motions, but I don't really feel anything.

As I climb out of the canyon back up onto the ridge, I can smell them. They may be smarter than they used to be, but the Zs still stink.

The land has gotten more desolate, the juniper shrubs pretty much gone and bits of grass and weeds the only thing left to cling to life in the reddish, sandy soil.

When the first group of about six Zs appears in front of me, I smile. They are acting like Zs used to act, single-minded and uncoordinated, jaws snapping as they snarl and reach for me. These are clearly from the tourist zombie horde that first chased June and me down into the canyon with their shorts and cameras dangling from their necks and a few with fanny packs on.

I turn and see the second group stumble onto the trail from behind a large boulder. They are not acting the same. I mean, sure, they want to eat me, they've got those yellow eyes, rags for clothes, and beat-to-shit bodies, but there is clearly intent in their eyes and they are silent.

The silence, honestly, is enough to freak me out a little bit. Zs aren't quiet. They are unquenchable hunger machines, stupid and relentless and noisy. But a quiet Z is another thing. And a group of quiet Zs cooperating with the "acting normal" Zs is downright terrifying.

"I don't want to fight you guys," I say, pulling my gun and pointing it at the silent group. There is an older Z there, not in terms of age, she was probably young when she died, but in terms of her leathered and desiccated appearance. She looks most like the Z at the center of the pod that followed us from the cell tower treehouse and confronted us out in the 40s.

She's tall, all leathery skin and long limbs, her dirty hair used to be blond, and she's wearing dark shorts and a tank top that used to be white.

It's not lost on me that the central Z at the 40s was a woman and the one I suspect to be central Z here is a woman. Maybe the Z-pods are matriarchal.

"I will kill you," I say as they shamble closer, my heart leaping into action as adrenaline dumps into my bloodstream. I don't have a lot of time and this is definitely a risk, but I need something to focus on for a few moments other than Dallas and June and Talia.

The leathery Z looks right in my eyes and I can feel a connection, almost the same kind of connection I would feel if I really looked into the eyes of a living person and they looked into mine.

The silent Zs stop and the noisy Zs go silent and stop too, but not all together. It's the leathery woman that stops first, several of the Zs with her taking a step forward before shambling back.

"Let me pass," I say. "None of us have to die today."

Nothing happens except for sweat trickling down my back and the distant call of a raven echoing across the dry land, accompanied by my heart thumping in my chest. None of us move. No one makes a sound. The Z and I just stare at each other as I point my gun at her head.

This has to be a survival instinct. We saw it at the cell tower treehouse when we dropped the bomb—the Zs somehow figured out what it was and started moving away. And maybe that makes sense, that a survival instinct is one of the first aspects of an intelligent mind.

As the thought gels in my mind, I smile. This means the pods will be smarter in their attacks, but they will also care about survival, and that could help.

"Hasn't there been enough death?" I ask. I'm not really talking to that leathery Z, per se, but to the apocalypse. The Zs aren't human, that is clear, but they aren't really dead either, the fungus inside of them animating them, organizing them, using them. Hasn't the fungus had enough death?

It doesn't take long for the pod to give me its answer. They snarl in unison and all lunge at me. Their answer is a resounding "no."

I fire and am moving as soon as I pull the trigger and not aware if I hit the suspected leader. I scramble down the slope off the trail, using my bat as a kind of walking stick to control my slide and holster my gun.

They don't follow, but I see the leathery one watching me with clear eyes, and despite the heat, I feel a chill. Part of her left cheek is now hanging ragged. My bullet did hit her but not in a way that mattered.

We lock eyes for a moment, and I consider trying to finish the job just so I can see what happens to the pod. Maybe nothing would. Maybe they would revert without their matriarch. It's information worth having.

It's so strange, but I once again feel a kind of connection looking into those yellowed eyes. Like there's something behind them now, something besides unending hunger and need, something I recognize.

The moment doesn't last long before I turn away without doing anything. Maybe it's the sense of connection that stops me from firing. In any case, I have other priorities. I have to catch up to June and try to heal the rift between us. I have to meet Talia on the bridge and hope her raging ego brings her there with Dallas alive and intact. I have to hope that she was lying and hasn't taken over Phantom Ranch already. And I have to figure out how to survive the fight with Talia and walk away being able to live with myself.

I look back up the slope. "Bye," I say to the Z staring at me and giving it a silly wave. "I hope we never meet again."

I walk carefully along the loose soil and quickly find signs of June's passage and just follow it.

I may be a lone survivor again and I may have the odds stacked against me, but at least I managed to make the impossible choice and I have a purpose and a mission.

It's not a lot, but any purpose, any mission in an apocalypse.

More adventure, an unthinkable problem, and more Woody and June awaits you in... *Woody and June versus the Reunion*. Available 3/6/2024.

To stay abreast of all things Woody and June, head over to WoodyAndJune.com and sign up for my e-mail newsletter and don't miss out on a thing! Plus, you'll get a free ebook that includes "Park's Law of the Apocalypse," a newsletter-exclusive story in the world of Woody and June.

𝕏𝕏𝕏 𝕏𝕏 𝕏𝕏𝕏

WOODY AND JUNE VERSUS THE THE REUNION

Is Love and Understanding Enough?

Woody Beckman and June Medina defied the odds and found each other in post-zombie-apocalypse Arizona and made the friend of a lifetime in the free-spirited Dallas. No longer go-it-alone survivors, they now face the future together with something to lose. Each other.

Everything changes, but for Woody, June, and Dallas it happens all at once with Dallas getting captured, the Zs starting to act intelligently, June leaving to try to fight a war by herself, and Woody experiencing some disturbing physical changes.

With time running out can Woody and June find their way back to each other and rescue Dallas before it's too late?

A story of adventure and love and taking things (even the apocalypse) in stride.

BEFORE YOU GO

Before you go, my book, *Bits, Bites, and Rarities: The Worlds of Robert J. McCarter* is a fantastic introduction to my series and worlds. It's only available to my newsletter subscribers, and the price is the best part. It's free!

This action-packed book contains 15 stories, is 750+ pages long, and has 4 exclusive stories that are not available anywhere else, including "Park's Law of the Apocalypse," a story in the world of Woody and June you can't read anywhere else.

Get it today at *RobertJMcCarter.com/newsletter*

ABOUT THE AUTHOR

Robert J. McCarter is the author of more than ten novels and over a hundred short stories. He is a regular contributor to *Pulphouse Fiction Magazine* and his short fiction has also appeared in *The Saturday Evening Post, Andromeda Spaceways Inflight Magazine, Everyday Fiction*, and numerous anthologies.

Robert writes in a variety of genres from contemporary fantasy to science fiction and just about everything in between. His diverse background–including a career in software engineering, growing up on a ranch riding horses, and acting–colors the stories he tells.

He lives in the mountains of Arizona with his amazing wife and his ridiculously adorable dogs.

Find out more at:
RobertJMcCarter.com

BOOKS BY ROBERT J. MCCARTER

WOODY AND JUNE VERSUS THE APOCALYPSE

For a great deal, pick up *Woody and June Versus the Apocalypse* a volume at at time!

Woody and June Versus the Apocalypse: Volume 1 (Episodes 1 - 7)

- Woody and June versus the Wannabe Warlord
- Woody and June versus the Fungus-Head Zombies
- Woody and June versus the Grand Canyon
- Woody and June versus the Ex
- Woody and June versus the Third Wheel
- Woody and June versus Phantom Company
- Woody and June versus the Daring Rescue

Woody and June Versus the Apocalypse: Volume 2 (Episodes 8 - 12)

- Woody and June versus the Chase
- Woody and June versus Two Guns
- Woody and June versus Winslow
- Woody and June versus the Infection
- Woody and June versus the Siege

Woody and June Versus the Apocalypse: Volume 3 (Episodes 13 - 17)

- Woody and June versus the Pod

- Woody and June versus the Impossible Choice
- Woody and June versus the Reunion
- Woody and June versus the Standoff
- Woody and June versus the End

Find out more at WoodyAndJune.com

NEUTRINOMAN & LIGHTNINGIRL: A LOVE STORY

For a great deal, pick up *Neutrinoman & Lightningirl: A Love Story* a season at at time!

Season 1 (Omnibus edition of Episodes 1 - 3)

- Meteor Attack!
- Toxic Asset
- Protocol X

Season 2 (Omnibus edition of Episodes 4-6)

- Off Book
- Hard Times
- Elemental Factors

Find out the latest at Neutrinoman.com

For a complete list of books, go to RobertJMcCarter.com/books

www.ingramcontent.com/pod-product-compliance
Lightning Source LLC
Chambersburg PA
CBHW020603130626
46552CB00007B/3022